THE MYSTERY OF THE
BLUE ARROWS

For Gaëlle Imbert

10 9 8 7 6 5 4 3 2 1

British Library Cataloguing in Publication Data available.

ISBN 1 84270 251 3

This book has been printed on acid-free paper

THE MYSTERY OF THE
BLUE ARROWS

Story by Chuck McKee
Pictures by David McKee

Andersen Press · London

Richard and Lucinda were playing noisily. Their mother didn't like it.

"I think you should take them for a walk," Mum said to Dad.

"Someone has painted a blue arrow on the wall," said Lucinda.

"Come on, Dad, let's see where it leads," said Richard.

"There's another arrow," said Lucinda a little later.
"Right, where's the next one?" said Richard.

"Who do you think painted them?" asked Lucinda.
"Someone who didn't want to get lost," said Richard.

"I think someone left them for his friends to follow," said Lucinda.

"Perhaps we shouldn't follow them," said Dad.
"Don't be silly," said Richard. "We can walk this way if we want to, arrows or no arrows."

"It could be a treasure hunt," said Lucinda. "One person goes ahead and leaves arrows for the others to follow then they race to find the treasure."

"It's more likely to be real robbers leaving a trail to real treasure," said Richard.
"We can find the treasure and spend it," said Lucinda.

"I'll buy a bicycle," said Richard.
"So will I," said Lucinda. "Then we won't have to go for a walk, we can ride."

"I don't think it's treasure," said Dad. "Anyone could follow the arrows and find it."

"What if it's robbers?" said Richard. "They could be hiding, waiting to leap out on people who follow the arrows and rob them."

"Well we haven't anything so they can't rob us," said
Lucinda.

"I have," said Dad.
"What – money?" said Richard.
"Yes," said Dad.
"Good, we can have an ice cream," said Lucinda.

"The arrows could have been left by someone who's been kidnapped," said Richard.
"Let's rescue them and get the reward," said Lucinda.

"That sounds dangerous," said Dad. "Perhaps we should go another way."
"Don't worry, Dad," said Lucinda. "We'll look after you."

"Maybe we'll be kidnapped," said Richard. "Dad will have to pay to get us back."
"Dad's with us. Mum would have to pay," said Lucinda.

"I think Mum would prefer to let them keep us so that she could have some peace and quiet," said Dad.

"It's an expedition going around the world," said Richard.
"That's a long way," said Lucinda.
"Yes, we have to be home by teatime," said Dad.

"It's a monster trying to trap his tea," said Richard.
"Monsters aren't bright enough to leave arrows, silly," said
Lucinda.

"Then it's a witch looking for a Hansel and Gretel to eat," said Richard.
"You're not a Hansel and Gretel," said Dad.
"A Richard and Lucinda are just as good for witches," said Lucinda.

"Stop frightening me," said Dad. "There could be anything in these woods."

"A giant," said Richard, "who wants to grind our bones to make his bread."

"FEE FI FO FUM!" growled the children together.

"Enough," said Dad. "I'm not going any further."
"Silly," said Lucinda. "Well wait there while we look over this ridge. Oh no. It's the end of the trail."
"I don't believe it," said Richard.
"What is it? What is it?" said Dad.

"Nothing much," said Richard. "Just an empty blue paint can and a brush."